LOS ANGELES UNIFIED SCHOOL DISTRICT

DEMCO

Chester
A Raccoon

by Bonnie Highsmith Taylor

Perfection Learning®

Dedication
For Lilly Denton

About the Author
Bonnie Highsmith Taylor is a native Oregonian. She loves camping in the Oregon mountains and watching birds and other wildlife. Writing is Ms. Taylor's first love. But she also enjoys going to plays and concerts, collecting antique dolls, and listening to good music.

Ms. Taylor is the author of several Animal Adventures books, including *Kip: A Sea Otter* and *Roscoe: A North American Moose*.

Cover photo: Corel professional photos

Image Credits: ©Michael H. Francis pp. 6, 11, 14–15, 32, 38–39, 48; ©Tom and Pat Leeson pp. 8, 12, 13, 19, 34–35, 37, 53; ©Steve Maslowski/Photo Researchers p. 29; ©Lynda Richardson/CORBIS p. 26

ArtToday (some images copyright www.arttoday.com); Corel professional photos title page, pp. 5, 9, 23, 24, 28, 44–45, 47, 54

Contents

The hollow in the tall fir tree was dark. Inside a female raccoon slept soundly. It was cold. Snow covered the ground.

The raccoon was not hibernating. But she had been asleep most of the winter.

She had mated in February. Her babies would not be born for a few more weeks. So she was still sleeping.

In the fall, she had eaten a lot of food. She had put on a lot of fat.

When the temperature dropped below freezing, she had found a hollow in a tree. She had curled up in a tight ball and had gone to sleep. She would live off her body fat until spring.

The male raccoon that she mated with had mated with other females. But he would have no part in raising the babies.

Outside the cozy hole in the fir tree, the wind blew. A herd of about 20 elk walked by. They were heading to the lake at the edge of the trees. They would feed on the new plants growing there. The elk cows were heavy with calves. But they would not be born for about two more months.

An osprey circled over the lake. It spotted a rainbow trout in the water. The osprey zoomed down. It caught the trout in its sharp talons. It flew to a tall tree and ate its catch.

Swallows flew around the lake. They had just returned from the south. They had spent the winter there. Other birds would return soon.

8

A coyote loped along below the raccoon's den. It sniffed the ground as it went. Under the snow, a mouse moved about. The coyote smelled it.

Suddenly, the coyote pounced! It caught the mouse. It swallowed it. Then it loped on, looking for more food.

From across the way, another coyote howled. Then a second joined in.

The coyote that was hunting stopped. It pointed its nose to the sky and answered. It howled loudly. It yapped. Then it howled again. The sound rang throughout the forest.

But inside the cozy den, the female raccoon did not stir. She slept very soundly. She was still too cold to wake up.

The female raccoon was nearly one year old. She weighed almost 11 pounds. She was about 32 inches long. Ten inches of that was her tail. She stood about 9 inches high at the shoulders.

The female was medium brown. She had darker rings around her tail. A black mask stretched across her eyes.

Male raccoon weigh 15 to 18 pounds. Females weigh 9 to 12 pounds. But they can be much larger, especially in captivity. There is a record of a raccoon that weighed over 60 pounds.

Raccoon have long, sharp claws for climbing. They have five toes on each foot. Unlike most animals, a raccoon walks on its entire foot like a human or a bear.

Raccoon have 40 teeth. They are very sharp.

Raccoon can be found in nearly all parts of the United States.

A few weeks passed. It grew a little warmer. The female raccoon stayed awake for longer periods of time.

If it does not warm up for a long time, raccoon often starve to death. They burn up all the fat they have stored.

The raccoon left the den where she had spent the winter. She was very hungry. In the nearby stream, she found food. Frogs, salamanders, and crayfish were her favorites.

Raccoon also eat berries, fruit, and nuts. In the fall, they eat lots of acorns. Acorns are low in protein. But they are high in fat and starches.

Raccoon love to raid farmers' cornfields. But they can be very destructive.

They also raid henhouses. They eat both the chickens and their eggs.

Raccoon rob birds' nests. They eat the young birds as well as the eggs.

Many people claim that raccoon wash their food before eating. But scientists explain that they are only acting out the instinct to search for food in water.

Raccoon search for food in water without even looking. They have a strong sense of touch. They have thousands of nerve endings in the skin of their front feet. Their sense of touch is better than humans have in their fingers.

The female raccoon ate her fill for several days. Then she searched for a place to have her babies.

She finally found the right place. It was a large hollow in a partly dead tree. The hollow was about 20 feet above the ground. For several days, the female slept in the hollow.

Then early one morning, she gave birth to three babies. Chester was the only male. He weighed about 4 ounces. He was nearly 9 inches long. That included his tail, which was a little over 2 inches long.

The other babies were a little smaller. The young raccoon's eyes and ears were tightly closed. They had very little fur. But their masks and the rings on their tails were already visible.

The babies squirmed in the nest. What a racket they made!

Baby raccoon are seldom quiet. They whine and chatter constantly unless they are asleep.

The mother raccoon cleaned her babies. Then she curled around them and let them nurse.

Chester's tiny paws pushed against his mother's stomach as he nursed. This made the milk come faster. His two sisters did the same. The milk foamed on the babies' mouths. It was warm and sweet.

When their stomachs were full, the babies fell asleep.

Raccoon are very good mothers. They will fight an animal of any size to protect their babies.

* * * * * * * *

In less than a week, Chester and his sisters were crawling around in the nest. Their chatter never stopped.

When the babies slept, the mother raccoon went hunting. In the streams and

ponds, she found crayfish and frogs. Sometimes she even caught fish. She ate lots of insects. She loved beetles.

Raccoon will even eat *carrion*, or dead animals.

The mother raccoon didn't stay away from her nest for very long. A pine marten, fisher, or bobcat could kill and eat her babies.

Pine marten

Even adult raccoon have enemies. Mountain lions and wolves kill raccoon. But man is their greatest enemy.

Raccoon have been hunted for their furs for many years. They are trapped or shot. Most hunters only want their furs. But some people eat their meat.

Hunters use dogs for hunting raccoon. Raccoon cannot outrun dogs. They cannot run much faster than 15 miles an hour. So they usually climb trees to escape.

Raccoon are very good climbers. Sometimes they come down trees headfirst if they are in a hurry.

Raccoon lived in places where early settlers made their homes.

Captain John Smith wrote about raccoon in his reports. He described them as animals that "look much like badgers. But lie in trees like squirrels."

Native Americans used raccoon fur for clothing. They traded the pelts to early settlers for guns and other things.

The name *raccoon* may have come from a Native American word for the animal, *Arakun*.

The settlers used the pelts for hats, coats, and robes to use when riding in sleighs. Before paper money was made, pelts were used for money.

In the 1920s, many raccoon were killed. Raccoon fur coats were popular, especially with college students.

In the 1950s, millions of coonskin caps were sold. Kids wanted to look like Walt Disney's Davy Crockett.

Boy with coonskin hat

The baby raccoon spent their days sleeping, nursing, and squirming. When they were awake, they were seldom still or quiet.

The little ones nursed and whimpered. Their mother made soft churring sounds. These sounds let the babies know that she was near and they were safe.

Raccoon make many different sounds. They hiss, whine, and churr. They make one sound that is like a bark or a cough.

When they are angry, raccoon growl and snarl. One sound that adult raccoon make is like the sound of a screech owl.

All around the forest and meadow, new plants and grass grew. Leaves formed on most of the trees. Birds built nests. Some had already laid their eggs.

On warm days, the female raccoon climbed out of the tree hollow. She lay on a high limb in the sun. She usually did not hunt until after dark.

As she lay on a limb dozing one morning, she heard a sound below. She looked down. A mother black bear ambled along. Two cubs waddled behind her. As the cubs followed their mother, they made snuffling noises.

Just below the raccoon, the cubs stopped. They began to tumble with each other. They wrestled and squealed.

Their mother stopped. She watched her cubs awhile. Then she was ready to move on. She grunted. The cubs paid no attention. The female raccoon watched from her overhead perch.

Again, the mother bear grunted. Still, the cubs played.

The mother bear moved closer to her cubs. She swatted each one with the flat of her paw. The cubs scrambled to their feet. The mother moved on through the forest. The cubs followed.

The female raccoon went back to sleep.

After a while she was wakened by her babies whimpering. She went inside the hollow and nursed them. Then she cleaned them. She licked the urine and feces from their bodies. This had to be done to keep the den clean. If the den became foul, the babies could get sick and die.

Raccoon can have fleas, ticks, lice, mange mites, and internal worms. They also can carry distemper and rabies. These are common animal diseases.

It is important for mother raccoon to keep themselves and their babies very clean.

At dusk, the female raccoon climbed down from the tree. She looked all around. It was safe.

She headed for the nearby creek. She reached her long front legs into the water. She felt under rocks with her front paws. She found some snails and mussels. She ate some water insects. Then under some old bark, she found several beetles. She even ate some grass.

When she had stuffed herself, she started back to her den.

Other animals stirred about in the dark. A porcupine nibbled on the bark of a pine sapling. The raccoon stayed far away from it. A mink hunted mice in the meadow.

From overhead, a large great horned owl swooped down. Seconds later, it rose into the air. It grasped a rabbit in its claws. It was taking the rabbit to the nest where its mate sat on three eggs. They would have a feast.

The baby raccoon began to whimper and wiggle around in the den when their mother returned.

The mother had filled her stomach. Now the babies would fill theirs.

Chapter 4

Chester's eyes were open! He was three weeks old. He could see a little. He could almost make out his mother and sisters.

It would take a while before his eyesight was strong. His sisters' eyes opened a day or two later.

The babies nursed more often as they got older. They stayed awake for longer periods. And they played! They played until they fell into a heap. They were all tired out.

When Chester was four weeks old, he weighed a little over 1 pound. He was about 13 inches long. His sisters were just a little smaller.

Their mother was very busy taking care of her family. Several times Chester tried to climb out of the tree hollow. But his mother always pulled him back.

One day, the mother returned from hunting to find a pine marten climbing up the tree. In a frenzy, she started up the tree after the marten. She hurried as fast as she could. She growled and snarled fiercely.

The marten froze. It could not go back down the tree. And it was no match against an angry mother raccoon.

The marten moved to the end of a branch. It looked over its shoulder and snarled at the raccoon. Then it made a big leap through the air. It landed on a branch about 6 feet away. Down the tree it went, headfirst.

By the time the mother raccoon reached her nest, the marten was out of sight.

The female raccoon sniffed her babies all over. She made soft chattering sounds. She cleaned them. As they nursed, she nuzzled them with her nose. Her babies were safe.

The babies were growing fast. Chester hated staying in the nest. It was dark. And there was not enough room to wrestle with his sisters.

He tried and tried to sneak out. But his mother always grabbed him by the back of the neck. Then she carried him back inside.

One day, the mother raccoon was outside the den. She was lying on a limb, sound asleep. She was just below the tree hollow.

Chester hung out the opening as far as he could. Very silently, he slid out onto the limb by his mother. In no time, his two sisters followed.

The mother raccoon awoke. She chattered at her babies. She may have been saying, "Be careful, now. Don't fall."

From then on, the babies were allowed to climb outside. They could sleep on branches of the tree, especially on hot days.

Males and females without young often sleep on tree branches. Instead of using hollows, they sometimes sleep on the ground. They move to a new place almost daily.

Nursing females and their young stay in one place longer. A hollow tree is warmer and safer for the babies.

The mother raccoon decided it was finally time to move her family. The babies were growing too large for the den. They needed to be where they could exercise.

She waited until the babies were asleep. Then she went house hunting. She

searched the forest at the edge of a swamp. She found a pile of logs. They had piled up when the water had been high two or three years before.

One large log was hollow. Huckleberry bushes grew in front of the opening. The den would be well-hidden. It would be a perfect place for her family.

The mother waited until dark. Then she moved her babies. She carried each one down the tree by its neck.

Chester squirmed and squealed as she carried him. He wanted loose. But his mother held him tighter. He squealed even louder.

Once there, Chester liked his new home. He crawled around inside. He sniffed it all over. The smells were all new to him. He smelled mice, frogs, and rabbits.

There was room to play with his sisters. And when he looked out the opening, he could see the meadow and the marsh. Yes, this would be a good home, Chester decided.

Chester and his sisters were four
months old. It was time to be weaned.
Chester didn't like the idea one bit. He
enjoyed filling his stomach with warm,
sweet milk. He liked being close to his
mother.

The three young raccoon spent hours
each day playing. They were never still
for a moment.

Raccoon are very playful. Some people think they make good pets when they are young. It is not a good idea to make pets of wild animals, though.

Raccoon are probably the most popular pet among wild animals. People who have had pet raccoon usually get rid of them when the animals get older. Raccoon often become cranky and mean.

And they are very destructive.

Chester loved to play in water. As he played, he ate insects that swam.

The first time Chester tried to catch a crayfish, he got his paw pinched. He squealed loudly. His mother came running. She comforted him by letting him nurse. And she nuzzled him with her nose.

It wasn't long before Chester and his sisters were good hunters. But they were not as good as their mother. They were still learning.

During the summer, the raccoon ate huckleberries, elderberries, and wild plums. They also feasted on frogs, earthworms, and birds' eggs. Chester hadn't caught a frog yet. But he had tried many times.

One day Chester and his sisters tasted something new. It was corn!

It was just before daybreak. They had followed their mother across the meadow, through an oak grove. They crawled under a fence and into a cornfield. The

young raccoon had never traveled so far.

The mother raccoon stood on her hind legs. She tore an ear of corn from a stalk. She dropped it on the ground. Then she tore off several more ears. She began to eat one of the ears of corn.

Chester moved close to her. He sniffed. He licked the milky juice on her mouth. It was good.

He began to chew on an ear of corn. His sisters did the same. They squealed and fought as they ate the delicious food. They had never tasted anything so good.

The raccoon ate until they could hold no more.

It was dawn when the raccoon family started across the field. They headed toward the fence.

Suddenly, a loud noise rang out. Chunks of dirt flew up just behind the raccoon. They ran as fast as they could!

Chester's heart beat wildly in his chest. He did not see the farmer with the gun. He only heard the frightening sound.

The raccoon were deep in the oak grove before they stopped running. The mother climbed a tree. Chester and his sisters followed. They stayed in the tree until night.

Finally, it was dark. They went back to their hollow log near the marsh. The raccoon family had been lucky—that time.

✳ ✳ ✳ ✳ ✳ ✳ ✳ ✳

In the fall, the berries were gone. But the wild grapes were ripe. And raccoon love grapes. Nuts were also plentiful.

Chester was getting better at catching frogs.

Several times in the fall, Chester heard the sound of guns again. The sound frightened him.

Hunting season had begun. Hunters were shooting deer. Once, Chester even saw a human.

Chester was curled up on a high limb. He was fast asleep. His mother and sisters were sleeping on limbs too.

The frightening sound rang out. It echoed through the forest. Chester jerked awake.

A human was walking through the forest. He was carrying a gun. He had shot at a deer. But he had missed. The deer had run away.

The hunter walked past the tree where the raccoon were. He did not see them.

For a long time, Chester held his breath. He was glad when the hunter was out of sight.

Chapter 6

The days grew colder. Leaves turned red and gold. Some fell from the trees. Nearly all the wildflowers were finished blooming for the year.

Many birds flew south for the winter. Small animals went into burrows. They would stay there until spring.

Deer and elk grew their thick winter coats. Black bears looked for dens. There

they would hibernate. And they would give birth during the winter.

Chester weighed nearly 15 pounds. He was strong and healthy. His sisters were still a little smaller than he was.

Often Chester went off alone. He spent his days sleeping in brush piles. Or he found a high limb in a tree.

Sometimes, he stayed away for a day or two at a time. But then he returned to his family. He was not ready to be on his own yet.

Chester would not find a mate until he was nearly two years old. His sisters would mate when they were about a year old. The mother raccoon would mate again in late winter. Her next litter would be born in the spring. By then, her first family would be gone.

Chester stuffed himself every night. He ate as much as he could hold. He had to put on a lot of fat. He needed enough to last through the cold winter.

One night, Chester was busy searching in the water for food. He was staring off into space. He swished around in the water with a paw. He turned over rocks, looking for something to eat.

It was very cold and quiet. Chester's mind was on one thing. And that was food!

Suddenly, a coyote crawled out of a thicket. He had been watching the raccoon for a while. Before Chester knew it, the coyote pounced.

Chester had never been attacked by a predator before. But at once, he whirled about to face the coyote. Their growls and snarls rang out in the night air. They fought fiercely.

Finally, Chester was able to break free of the coyote's grasp. He darted to a tree growing on the bank. He was up the tree in a flash.

The coyote jumped at the tree trunk. He showed his teeth and growled. It was nearly half an hour before he gave up and trotted away.

Chester lay on a limb for a long time. He was breathing hard. And he was cold. At last, he curled up in a tight ball close to the trunk of the tree. He stayed there until morning.

* * * * * * * *

The colder it got, the more sluggish Chester felt. It was time for the raccoon family to hole up for the winter.

The mother raccoon found a good hollow in a tall ash tree. It was big and warm. The whole family could den together. The family would stay together until the mother had another litter.

The raccoon would sleep for days at a time. If it turned warm, they would come out of the den for short periods.

But when they did, they would not move about much. That would burn up their stored fat. Then they might not make it through the winter.

The snow fell. Strong winds blew through the forest. The winds were so strong that some trees fell.

The pond and the creek froze over. Deer and elk had to break the ice with their hooves to get a drink.

Many animals would not make it through the winter. They could not find food.

Coyotes hunted mice under the snow. They hunted deer in packs. But deer were not always easy to kill. So the coyotes howled mournfully when they went to bed hungry.

But inside the snug den, the raccoon family did not hear the strong winds blowing. They did not hear limbs crashing to the ground. And they did not hear the coyotes howling.

They were warm and cozy as they slept the winter away.

* * * * * * * *

Spring came at last. Each day was warmer. The ice melted from the pond and the creek. Leaves formed on trees. Grass and wildflowers sprouted.

And inside the tree hollow, the raccoon family awoke.

Chester's mother and sisters had mated. In a few weeks, they would have their young.

It was time for Chester to leave. He was able to take care of himself now. In another year, he would mate.

In his lifetime of about ten years, Chester would father many baby raccoon. But he would never know these babies.

His sisters also left. The raccoon family would probably never see one another again.

Chester wandered for several days. He moved through the woods and across several open fields. At last, he came to a valley. Near a river was a big meadow at the edge of a forest. Fir, pine, maple, and oak trees grew there.

It was an old forest. It would be easy

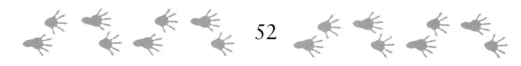

for Chester to find hollow trees.

Not far away were some farms. Fruit orchards would produce apples, cherries, and plums. And later in the summer, melons and corn would be plentiful.

What a perfect place for a raccoon. This would be Chester's new home.

Check out the World Wide Raccoon Web for raccoon facts, a picture gallery, raccoon in the news, and links to other sites.

www.loomcom.com/raccoons

✳   ✳   ✳   ✳   ✳   ✳   ✳